Invincible Voices
Short Shorts

with best wishes

Zoe ☺

Invincible Voices
Short Shorts

Zoe Antoniades

Front cover illustration by Athena Estrada

Matador
9 Priory Business Park,
Wistow Road, Kibworth Beauchamp,
Leicestershire. LE8 0RX
Tel: 0116 279 2299
Email: books@troubador.co.uk
Web: www.troubador.co.uk/matador
Twitter: @matadorbooks

ISBN 978 1788036 481

British Library Cataloguing in Publication Data.
A catalogue record for this book is available from the British Library.

Printed and bound by CPI Group (UK) Ltd, Croydon, CR0 4YY
Typeset in 12pt Aldine401 BT by Troubador Publishing Ltd, Leicester, UK

Matador is an imprint of Troubador Publishing Ltd

Zoe Antoniades was born in West London in 1973. She graduated from the University of Hull with a degree in English and Drama and later trained as a teacher at the Institute of Education.

Her Invincible Voices company provides creative writing workshops for young people where the stories in this publication have been brought to life.

Zoe has written the school story *Staircase to Nowhere* and a memoir *Tea and Baklavas* which won the Winchester Writers' Festival Memoir Prize and is published in Winchester University's *Best of 2015*.

www.zoeantoniades.com

Little voices made big

These stories are *for* children *by* children; they contain first-hand concepts that children want to read about because children have chosen to write them. With a skilled teacher and author, Zoe Antoniades, to guide them, the children are inspired to come up with their own ideas, then helped to shape, structure, organise and develop them so that they evolve into more professional pieces. The result of such an approach is a unique style, a hybrid product of adult and child's voice. The stories possess the spirit and originality of a child's creative ideas, but with the polish and flair of an experienced writer.

Invincible Authors

Zoe Antoniades
Alishbah Atif
Lily Beglin
Max Currie
Camron Dhillon
Sacha Doherty
Rehaan Gupta Chaudhary
Adam Hakiem
Rayan Haque
Neelay Kawol
Raja Khalid
Ariana Khan
Lakshmi Lakshmanan
Vijai Lakshmanan
Deeqa Mohamed
Ahmed Pasha
Anban Senthil Prabu
Thendral Senthil Prabu
Balraj Singh
Anisha Sirajudeen
Siddharth Sridhar
Adeline Veschi
Pavan Yadlapati

Contents

Jimmy Hero

By Adeline Veschi

Hi, I'm Jimmy Hero and I'm an awesome superhero. But before I start babbling on about all sorts, I will tell you a bit about myself. I wear large black-rimmed glasses, a milky-coloured jacket and a sapphire blue T-shirt with my initials 'JH' inside a diamond. It's actually my superhero logo, but no-one else knows that.

So what makes me a superhero? My super-cleverness. I once sat a Year Six paper and got top marks when I am only in Year One. That's right, I'm just five years old, but I have the brains of Einstein.

Today I'm in my treehouse (which is actually my Superspy HQ), brushing up on my forensics studies. But wait… what's that…? Someone moving around in the house next door? My friend Tina Transformer's house. But they're meant to be away on holiday aren't they? And who's that now, leaving through the back door in a black and white striped T-shirt? Hey! Wait! He's got a huge black bag slung over his shoulder. It's a burglar! What if it's Tina's spy kit in that bag?

Must act fast.

Quick as a flash, I abseil down the tree and dive through a secret panel in the fence. I'm in next door's garden now and the burglar's there too. He spots me and makes a run for it. But I leap on his back and grab onto his hair.

"Ouch! What you doing you little blighter?" he yells, shaking me off and bashing me out of the way with his sack.

"Ooof!" I cry.

He drops the sack and dashes over the fence. Little does he know, he's caught his trousers on a nail and a piece has ripped off. I can see his red spotty pants! Then, he disappears over the other side of the fence.

At least I've saved Tina's stuff. The sack will be evidence for starters. I retrieve the trouser fabric too. And what's this on my palms? Strands of his hair. His actual DNA! More evidence!

I bolt back to my place and find Mum in the kitchen.

"Next door's been burgled! Call the police, quick!" I say.

Mum grabs the phone, dials 999 and explains everything.

Before we know it, Tina's garden is overrun with uniformed men. Mum and I go over to speak with them. I'm waving the DNA evidence at them, but all they want to do is talk to my mum.

"When...? blah, blah, blah... Where...? blah, blah, blah... What...? blah, blah, blah..."

Finally they notice me.

"What you got there, son?" the chief detective questions me.

I proudly present him with the black sack, the fabric and the hair strands.

The chief detective smiles. "Send this straight to forensics," he says.

My evidence all points to the notorious criminal, Jack the Bad.

"We'll soon have him behind bars, thanks to you, sonny," says the detective.

All in a day's work, I think to myself. Because I'm Jimmy Hero, and I'm an awesome superhero.

The Come-to-Life Comic

By Anban and Thendral Senthil Prabu

It was a rainy Sunday, just like any other, and Aaron McCawley was in his bedroom reading the latest edition of Aero-Man Saves the Day, a comic for children who like superheroes. He knew he should really be doing his homework, so he put down the comic and picked up his spellings. That was when he heard a mysterious cry for help. It seemed to be coming from the comic.

Aaron picked it up again and turned the pages, only to find Discus-Dan chasing Aero-Man. This was strange, because Aero-Man was usually in control as he was the hero. Discus-Dan was trying to capture Aero-Man with his hover-discs – small discs that flew overhead and released a net over their victims. But, whenever Discus-Dan kept firing his hover-discs, Aero-Man, who was super agile, would somersault away.

Unfortunately for Aero-Man, instead of jumping to the left, he dived to the right and eventually got caught. He struggled inside the net yet still somehow managed to bundle Discus-Dan. A full fight broke out. With all the panicking and struggling they both tumbled out of the pages only to find themselves in Aaron's bedroom. They gazed up at Aaron who stared down at them in disbelief.

"Aaahhh it's a giant! Run for your lives!" they both shrieked, for although Aaron was just a boy, he seemed enormous in comparison to the two tiny figures.

Aaron couldn't believe that the superheroes from his favourite comic had come alive and were now running around in his bedroom like a pair of wild things. The two tiny figures made a dash for it, out of the bedroom and along the hallway.

"Come back!" Aaron called after them.

He looked all over the upstairs of the house for the two escaped characters – in his mum and dad's bedroom, in the study and finally in the bathroom. He pulled back the shower curtain where he found Aero-Man and Discus-Dan cowering together.

Aaron removed the net from Aero-Man and disarmed Discus-Dan by taking away his remaining hover-discs. He then carefully picked them both up and took them back to his room.

"Calm down, please," remarked Aaron, trying to sound like a grown-up.

Aero-Man and Discus-Dan stopped and stared at the enormous giant.

"What on earth is going on?" asked Aaron.

"Fine, I'll tell you," breathed Aero-Man, remembering he was meant to be a hero after all. "For some reason, this villain..." he began.

"I'm no villain!" objected Discus-Dan. "Let *me* tell you what happened…"

"If you insist," said Aero-Man folding his arms.

"Aero-Man always gets to be the hero and I find it really unfair," complained Discus Dan.

"So you think that trying to capture me makes it alright?" protested Aero-Man.

"Well yes, because then I get to save the day," explained Discus-Dan.

"But I'm a hero. If you catch me, that just makes you a villain, doesn't it?" mocked Aero-Man.

"Er... um... well... so what?" mumbled Discus-Dan, not sure what else to say.

"Guys, we need to fix this," sighed Aaron.

The two heroes turned their heads.

"I've figured a way to sort out the problem," he continued.

The two superheroes were all ears.

"So, Discus-Dan says he wants to save the day like Aero-Man," said Aaron.

Discus-Dan and Aero-Man nodded.

"Ok then, all we have to do is draw a line down the centre of the comic and split it into two zones. One side for each of you."

"I like it!" smiled Discus-Dan.

"Sounds reasonable," mumbled Aero-Man.

Aaron got a pencil, and with his ruler, he drew a line so the two characters could share the stories more fairly.

"Thanks!" cheered Discus-Dan leaping back into the pages, followed by Aero-Man.

Soon things became much better. The line Aaron

drew really worked and Discus-Dan and Aero-Man never argued again. Each night they would pop out of the comic and sit on Aaron's pillow and tell him all about their latest adventures.

Charlie's Adventure

By Vijai Lakshmanan

"I want to go to the museum," pleaded Charlie. He had been bugging his parents all month about it.

"I can't take you now, I'm off to bingo," said Mum grabbing her bingo card.

"Go and watch TV like a good boy, I'm off to work," muttered Dad picking up his briefcase.

Charlie dragged himself over to the couch, sat down and tapped a random number into the TV control: 555. Seconds later, the most ear-splitting noise vibrated around the room. BEEEEEEEEEP!!!

The four-seater couch turned into a two-seater train carriage. Charlie was speechless and wondered what was going on.

"Next stop, South Kensington. Alight here for the Natural History Museum."

It sounded like a real voice, not the usual automated one.

Charlie looked around and found the carriage was deserted. He was getting freaked out. Trains couldn't talk. Could they? Charlie shuddered with fear.

When the train came to a stop, Charlie thought he'd better get off. He cautiously stepped down from the train and it swiftly took off again behind him.

"Oh no! The couch has gone with the train!" realised Charlie. Oh well, there was not much he could do about that now. He hoped Mum and Dad wouldn't be too cross about it.

Charlie looked around him. The platform was crowded with people all rushing and pushing. He felt dazed and confused.

"I want to go home," he cried.

Fortunately a policeman heard him. He found Charlie looking lost on the platform.

"It's alright now. How did you get here?" asked the gentle policeman.

"I… I… I'm not sure… I don't know if you'd even believe me if I tried to explain…" stammered Charlie.

The policeman gave Charlie a mysterious knowing smile. There was a twinkle in his eye too.

"I may understand more than you think," he murmured.

Charlie was a little suspicious of this mysterious man, but he seemed so friendly and he was a policeman after all.

"You want to go to the museum, don't you?" asked the policeman.

"How did you…?" started Charlie.

"We need not be concerned about such things now," said the policeman. "As your parents can't take you, I will."

"But… but…how…?" Charlie was even more baffled. This unusually clever policeman really did seem to know a lot.

Then the policeman caused something even more unexpected to happen. He tapped a code into his walkie-talkie and in a flash they were zooming down a dark narrow tunnel.

Before Charlie knew it, he found himself standing by the policeman's side in the museum itself. They were in front of a massive skeleton. Its neck was so long, it couldn't fit inside the building. In fact, it went through a hole in the roof, so it appeared as if it was beheaded.

"Wow! That's an awesome Diplodocus! It's so real," marvelled Charlie.

"Charlie, you *are* aware it isn't alive," chuckled the policeman.

"I know that really," Charlie laughed too.

Several hours passed and Charlie and the policeman had a great time talking together about the dinosaurs.

"There's a Tyrannosaurus Rex… and there's a Brachiosaurus… and oh, I can't believe it, an Allosaurus too!" Charlie was having such a fantastic time, thanks to his new friend the policeman.

Only after all that, did Charlie think to look at his watch. He realised he had been away for hours.

"Oh no! I really should be getting back home. Will you help me find my way?" asked Charlie.

"I'll take you back to the train station," said the policeman. "The 555 train will be here soon."

"How did you know about that weird number?" asked Charlie.

The policeman smiled his mysterious, knowing smile once more, and there was that twinkle in his eye again.

"It's my secret number," he explained. The policeman handed Charlie his walkie-talkie. "Here, you can have this. I've got another one at the police station. Any time you need a friend, just tap 555 and I'll be there."

Charlie couldn't believe his luck. He wasn't sure how any of these strange happenings had occurred, but he didn't mind, because he'd had the best day ever at the museum and from now on, he would never be lonely again.

The Dinner Lady of Aylesbury School

By Lakshmi Lakshmanan

"Did you see how much homework we got today?" complained Jack.

"I know, Mr Smart gave us a whole pile of it," groaned Janet.

"I hate maths. I'm going to accidentally on purpose lose the worksheets," laughed Margaret.

Margaret, Janet and Jack were three good friends who were all in Year 5 at Aylesbury School. Margaret was really imaginative, but the other two thought her stories were nonsense.

"At least it's not too long till lunch. I can't wait to taste the dinner lady's delicious food," said Janet.

Janet and Jack loved the dinner lady, but Margaret really hated her. She thought that there was something very mysterious about her. She didn't trust her and always referred to her as the

Demon Dinner Lady behind her back. Janet and Jack were having none of it. They loved the food that she cooked. They ate it every lunchtime, even though they always became drowsy afterwards. Margaret always brought a packed lunch to school. However, the Demon Dinner Lady was always with them, whether they had packed lunch or school dinners, so there was no escape from her. She gave Margaret dirty looks all the time.

During maths, after they had handed in their homework from the previous day, Margaret thought about the Demon Dinner Lady. She wasn't sure why, but she had a bad feeling about what she might be up to. So she made an excuse to get out of the lesson.

"Sir, can I please go to the toilet?" she asked.

"You're meant to go at playtime," he sighed.

"But Sir, I'm really desperate," pleaded Margaret.

"Ok, but just this once," agreed Mr Smart.

Margaret dashed out of the classroom and along the corridor. She crept up to the dinner hall. Through the window she spied the Demon Dinner Lady throwing three eyeballs and five rotten eggs (including their shells) into a saucepan. Next she added what seemed like a ton of sugar (to sweeten it all up), followed by a cat's tail and a splodge of slug's slime. Lastly, she finished it all off with a squirt of toothpaste.

Just then, the bell rang for lunch and the Demon Dinner Lady looked up. That's when she spotted Margaret at the window. She reached for her wooden spoon, which was really a wand, and raised it in the air to a cast a spell. Margaret ran away just in time.

The Demon Dinner Lady chased her down the corridor but Margaret noticed she was struggling quite a bit to keep up, it was as if she was in pain. Margaret was tiring too, she had completely run out of breath and found herself cornered by the Demon Dinner Lady.

The Demon Dinner Lady put her hand to her head as if it ached. Margaret noticed that her face looked like rubber and it was creased around her forehead. The loose skin around the top of her head began to fall away. The Demon Dinner Lady cried in pain and peeled it all off, like a mask, to reveal her true self. Blood dripped from her scalp.

"I knew it!" exclaimed Margaret. "I knew you were hiding something. I always knew you were a witch!"

"You shouldn't have meddled in my business. There is no escape for you now," threatened the Demon Dinner Lady. She raised her wand again and directed it at Margaret. She closed in on the terrified girl, so close Margaret could feel her breath, which was as cold as ice.

"Not so fast," came a voice from the top of the corridor. It was Mr Smart. He ran up and grabbed the wand from the Demon Dinner Lady's grip. He threw it over to Margaret and she immediately cast a spell on the witch causing her to freeze.

Jack and Janet came running too.

"What's going on?" they chorused.

"Long story," sighed Margaret.

Jack and Janet gasped at the sight of the Demon Dinner Lady.

"Wow! So she really *is* a witch," said Janet.

"Sorry for not believing you," apologised Jack.

Mr Smart pulled out his mobile phone and dialled 911. The police arrived straight away. They confiscated the Demon Dinner Lady's wand for evidence and led her to a police car that was waiting on the playground. Hoards of children and staff had gathered around, trying to work out what was going on and spreading all sorts of rumours.

"None of this would have happened if you hadn't interfered," grimaced the Demon Dinner Lady as she was handcuffed and made to sit in the back of the car.

Margaret turned to Mr Smart. "Thank you for rescuing me, Sir," she said.

"Perhaps this will make you think twice about skipping class," he said sternly. But his frown turned into a smile as he added, "However, I think I can speak for Jack and Janet and the rest of the school when I say you also deserve a jolly good pat on the back."

Everyone laughed with relief, reassured that the doom of the Demon Dinner Lady had come to an end.

A Problem Shared

By Anban and Thendral Senthil Prabu

In a typical primary school, in a Year Two classroom just like any other, a six-year-old girl was having difficulties. Rosie was the name of this unhappy child; she had trouble with reading and writing.

She stared at the whiteboard but couldn't make out any of the words. Unfortunately for Rosie, she was a very shy girl who didn't like sharing her problems with anyone, not even her mum. Instead, she would make up elaborate excuses to get out of class.

That day, she put up her hand and said, "Miss, may I go to the toilet? My older brother locked the door, so I haven't had a chance to go yet."

Her teacher, who was won over by Rosie's cute large eyes, instantly replied, "Yes."

When Rosie returned, she was in for a surprise. Every week, someone from each class was chosen to write the newsletter with the headmaster, and this time, to Rosie's horror, the teacher picked her. Rosie, with no other choice, groaned as she followed the headmaster to his office along with some other, more cheerful, children.

The headmaster, Mr Ray, greeted the children and started discussing plans whilst handing out key points to follow. Rosie, using her excuse-making skills, told the headmaster she had a violin lesson and managed to sneak out.

At home time, Rosie dragged her feet and didn't feel much like chatting to her mother. As soon as they reached home, Rosie ran upstairs like a lightning bolt and flung herself onto her bed. Her mother was astonished. She softly opened the door to Rosie's room, only to find her sobbing.

"What is the matter darling?" asked her mother. "You're not usually like this."

"I… I… n…n… need… t… t… to write a…"

"Darling, don't splutter, can you try to speak more clearly?"

Rosie lifted her head and tried her best to control her voice. As clearly as she could, she explained to her mother why she was feeling upset.

"At school, I have trouble understanding anything. I can't even read the whiteboard. Then today, I was chosen to write the weekly newsletter and I had to go to the headmaster's office with some other children."

"And then...?" asked Rosie's mother, intrigued by her story.

"Then..." Rosie continued, "...when we went to his office, he gave us some paper which he said was for planning. After, he told us that we had to write a report. But I couldn't, because all the words on the paper started running into each other. So I made an excuse and ran away." Rosie wiped a tear from her cheek. "Are you angry Mummy?"

"No, no, no, not at all honey," replied her mother, although she was still trying to make sense of it all inside. Her mind was blown by what her daughter had said.

"But I'm rubbish at everything," cried Rosie.

"You might find reading difficult, but maybe you are good at something else. Everyone has their own special talent," her mother tried to reassure her.

"But I haven't. I'm useless. I just want to hide!" sobbed Rosie.

"Oh, don't say that, darling. You are a wonderful young girl. I wouldn't trade you for the world."

Rosie's mother felt terrible for her. She gently patted Rosie's back and stroked her hair. As she did so, she gazed around the room. There on the wall, was a painting that Rosie had done of the family all together at the park. It was fantastic, as were all of Rosie's pictures.

"That's it!" said her mother brightening up. "Why don't you try *drawing* your news report, like a comic – strip?"

Rosie smiled. It was a brilliant idea. She took out her colouring pencils and sketch book and got straight down to it. Within half an hour she had produced the most amazing presentation of a recent visit from The Happy Puzzle Company.

"That's amazing, darling," exclaimed Rosie's mother when she had finished.

Rosie couldn't wait to show the headmaster at school the next day. It was the first time, in a long time, that she was excited about going to school at all.

Standing proudly in the headmaster's office the next morning, Rosie and her mother presented the comic-strip report.

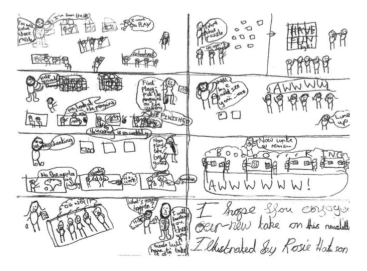

The headmaster was both stunned and extremely pleased all at once.

"This is amazing, Rosie Watson," said Mr Ray. "I think we should make you a permanent illustrator for the school newsletter from now on."

Rosie beamed with pride.

"Now run along to class while I have a little chat with your mummy," he said.

Rosie skipped happily to her classroom where she felt ready to take on anything.

It turned out that Mr Ray already knew something of Rosie's problems with reading and writing.

"Mrs Watson," he said. "I would like to set up a programme for your daughter to help her with her difficulties. We have a specialist member of staff who can work with her in a small group with her friends. We'll be keeping a closer eye on Rosie from now on."

"That is most reassuring. Thank you so much," smiled Rosie's mother.

"You're most welcome. We'll be in touch again soon," said the headmaster, showing her out.

On Friday, when the newsletter came out, Rosie became an instant celebrity. Everyone surrounded her, asking her to sign their copies. Everyone wanted to know this awesome artist. Everyone knew that Rosie was indeed a gifted child.

Runaway Cat

By Max Currie

There was once an adorable, cute, fluffy, ginger cat called Muffin. He lived at 87 Hartham Road, just outside of London, with his owner Max. Max thought Muffin was very lazy because he slept on his bed a lot.

However, Muffin didn't sleep all the time. Most nights he liked to sneak out and go on adventures after dark.

One night, Muffin decided to go out and catch mice. When he was prowling around in the back garden, he sensed something watching him. He froze on the spot with fear. He heard something snarling. Muffin turned to see a wild dog staring at him. This was a dog who was out to catch a cat who was out to catch mice.

Muffin dashed away from the dog at top speed, over walls and through miles and miles of alleyways, until at last he escaped from the ferocious hound. But when he looked around him, he realised that he was lost.

He looked around some more and noticed a house on the top of a hill. In the window of the house sat a large, fat, ginger cat observing his surroundings. The cat was a giant version of Muffin himself. He was called Felix and he was a spy cat. He had x-ray vision, a jetpack and a golden collar studded with gems. He crept down from the window ledge and padded softly over to Muffin.

"Is there anything I can do to help?" asked Felix.

"Yes please. You see, I'm lost and I can't get home," said Muffin.

Felix led Muffin to the top of the hill and used his long-distance vision to scan the area. Then, with his x-ray eyes, he looked through the walls of the houses until he spotted a boy sitting up on his bed, seeming as if he'd lost something.

"What does your owner look like?" asked Felix.

"He's nine years old, with blonde hair," explained Muffin.

"Does he have lots of toys on his bed too, like Mickey Mouse and Spongebob?" asked Felix.

"Yes that's him! That's my Max!" cried Muffin.

"Excellent. You can use my sat-nav and jetpack to get you home," offered Felix.

Felix strapped the jet pack on Muffin's back and the gem-studded collar, which contained the sat-nav, around his neck. He programmed it go to Max's house. Muffin was overjoyed. He was going home! He flew through the air like lightning. It was thrilling.

Back at 87 Hartham Road, Muffin was delighted to be reunited with Max. He hopped up onto the bed and Max tickled Muffin on his belly until he fell asleep… again!

But now we know that Muffin does not actually sleep all the time, we're bound to see him on another adventure again soon.

Attack of the Giant Spider

By Rayan Haque

In a small town called Smallville, there lived a small boy called George. For a small boy, he had a very big fear. Spiders!

One evening, he was sitting at home watching the news when a terrifying story came up. There had been a horrific incident at the local nuclear plant. A hairy black spider had fallen into the nuclear waste pit and reacted with the chemicals and atoms. There was an explosion and after that, the spider had emerged from the pit. Its DNA was altered by the nuclear reaction causing the spider to grow and grow to the size of a double-decker bus. The scientists evacuated the lab in terror, leaving the spider free to escape. The news report said that all they knew was that the spider was somewhere running wild in Smallville.

George gulped. That spider could be anywhere!

His greatest fears were confirmed when he heard a tap-tap-tapping at the window. He turned to look towards where the sound was coming from and saw a giant, monstrous spider glaring at him through the glass pane. Its eyes were the size of headlamps and they looked hungry. It continued to tap heavily at the window with its hairy black legs, until, with one great blow, the window shattered to pieces and the spider broke through.

George dashed to the door, tore it open and sped down the street like mad. When he dared to look behind, he found that the spider was scuttling after him furiously. Its sharp fangs gnashed ravenously. George felt certain that he would soon be devoured by this mutant beast.

"Heeeeelp! Heeeeelp!" screamed George.

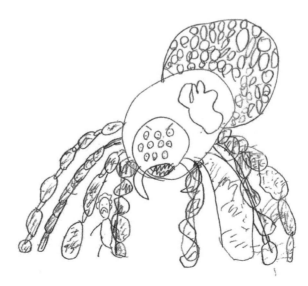

Luckily a pest control exterminator, who was on a nearby street looking for the spider, heard George's cries. He raced around the corner to find George running wildly towards him, his arms and legs flailing crazily. The spider was in hot pursuit and was growing in size. By the time the exterminator arrived on the scene, the spider was the size of a dinosaur.

The exterminator shouted, "HOLY TARANTULAS!" He flung himself to his car, and searched frantically for his best toxic anti-spider chemical formula and sprayed it over the spider's hairy head. The spider stopped but nothing else happened. George ran to safety and so did the exterminator.

The exterminator commanded George to get his best toxic anti-beast chemical formula. George gulped and muttered his fears to himself as he went to the car. He retrieved the deadly chemical but when he tried to hand it to the exterminator, the spider caged him with his big, hairy legs.

"Oh no, I'm dinner!" thought George.

The spider bit down so hard that its teeth sunk into the road. George dodged its jaws just in time and made a quick getaway.

George handed the formula to the exterminator who mixed it with the anti-spider spray from before.

"Now we have a super-anti-spider-beast formula!" the exterminator brandished the new upgrade.

He sprayed the spider again, but it still didn't work.

"Spray it in its mouth!" urged George.

The spider opened its jaws as if hungry for another dinner-bite.

"Now's your chance!" insisted George, more mad than scared now.

With one final spray, hundreds of super chemical particles rained into the spider's mouth. The colossal spider crumbled to smithereens.

"Wow! That was some ending!" marvelled the exterminator.

"You were awesome!" admired George.

"I couldn't have done it without you, boy," said the exterminator.

And for the first time in his life, George felt brave.

Buster's Escape

By Pavan Yadlapati

It was an ordinary sunny morning and an ordinary college day for teenage student Jack. Except, Jack wasn't just ordinary. He was a spy.

He was in the middle of a lesson when his watch bleeped. It was the hotline to Master-X. Something was not right. Jack excused himself from class and went to answer the call.

"What is it, Master-X?" asked Jack.

"Buster the Bank Robber has escaped again, and it can only mean bad news," said Master-X.

"I'm right on it," said Jack.

"You have to stop him. He's after the head of the Bank of England to get the gold. He's about to arrive right now!" exclaimed Master-X. "You'll need your jet pack," he continued, "because there are road works going on. An enormous hole in the main street, just down the road from the bank."

This gave Jack a brilliant idea…

When Jack arrived at the bank, everything was a total mess. It was as if a hurricane had blown through the place. All the customers and bankers lay on the floor in silence with their hands on their heads. Buster was busy filling a sack with money.

Jack snatched the bag and yelled, "You hoo, Buster! Come and get me!"

"What's going on? Who could that be?" said Buster, turning around in confusion. "Jack!!!" he cried.

In a rage, Buster chased after Jack. He was a really fast runner so Jack needed to use his jetpack. Jack led Buster towards the gigantic hole in the road. Buster was so fast, he couldn't stop in time. This was Jack's cunning plan. He wanted Buster to fall in. But, when Buster was just about at the edge of the hole, he grabbed onto Jack's ankle and flew up into the air with him.

"Ow!" cried Jack.

His plan had failed. But not for long. Jack activated his super spy watch. He used the voice control device to set his next plan into action.

"Go slippery slime!" he instructed the watch. The watch bleeped and a tremendous torrent of oozy, green, gooey, gungy, rotten slime gushed out. It ran down Jack's leg to his ankle. Buster's grip slipped away with the slime until he could hold on no longer.

"Whhhhhhooooooooah!"
cried Buster as he fell into
the great hole in the road.

Jack flew down
and clapped a pair of
handcuffs on Buster.

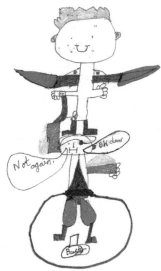

Crowds had gathered
in the street to watch and
everyone was peering
down into the hole to
get a better view of the
captured criminal. There
was a lot of cheering.

Jack felt exhausted but very pleased too. Buster
was miserable and struggled to break free. But this
time he was trapped good and proper.

The hotline to Master-X bleeped once again on
Jack's watch.

"Well done, Jack," said Master-X. "I hear you
have succeeded in your mission to defeat Buster.
Congratulations!"

"All in a day's work. Let's hope that's the last of
his evil crimes," said Jack.

"That's what *you* think," grumbled Buster.

Jordan Springs to Action

By Vijai and Lakshmi Lakshmanan

"It's now time to award the medal for the high-jump in our National Junior Athletics Championships," announced the commentator over the loud speaker. "All our young athletes have given a phenomenal performance today. It's been a tough competition, but there can only be one winner."

A hush fell amongst the crowd. On the bench, by the medal podiums, sat the hopeful contestants. Amongst them were the favourites for the high-jump. There was Steve, who was so powerful he was known as Steve Strong, and also Jordan, who was nicknamed Jumping Jordan because he was so springy.

"In third place…" declared the commentator, "we have Flexible Freddie!"

The crowd cheered as Freddie bounced over to the podium to be awarded his bronze medal.

Steve smirked at his rival Jordan. "You're next," he said.

"Let's just wait and see, shall we?" replied Jordan, confident he'd done well too.

"And in second place... please give a generous round of applause for our runner up... Steve Strong!"

"WHAT!!" yelled Steve.

"Don't be such a sore loser," smiled Jordan. He was really happy inside as he knew the gold medal was surely his now.

However, he wasn't to find out, because Steve, in his anger, was not heading over to the podium to collect the silver medal. Instead, he marched up to the table where the awards were on display, grabbed all the medals, including the gold one that was most likely Jordan's, dashed past the shocked judges and made a run for it before anyone could stop him.

The commentator fainted in shock, the judges fumed and the crowds gasped. Where had he disappeared to so quickly?

Jordan noticed a flash of something on the roof of the stadium. It was the medals glinting in the sunlight. Steve was up there!

Jordan felt a strange change come over him, as if a powerful surge of energy was boosting his body. He made a running jump for the top of the stadium and, to both his and the crowd's astonishment, he bounded up to the roof, realising for the first time that he had amazing superpowers.

Jordan landed on the domed roof in front of his rival.

"Stop! Thief! Hand back those medals," he ordered.

"How did you get here?" panicked Steve in confusion.

Jordan hardly knew himself, but there was no time to dwell on that now. "Never mind that," he said reaching out for the medals. But before he could get his hands on them, Steve backed away. Jordan went after him, but he tripped over a pipe and fell, enabling his obnoxious rival to make an escape.

But Jordan wasn't going to give up. Once more, that strange feeling came over him and he felt his feet itching to bound and leap. Almost automatically, as if his body was taking control of the situation, Jordan found himself soaring in a great arc through the air. He overtook his enemy and landed on the opposite side of the dome.

Steve Strong looked frantically around, wondering where Jordan had disappeared to. He was, in fact, hiding on the ledge beneath the roof, lying in wait for Steve.

Steve looked about for some way of escape. "Perhaps I could slide off the dome and climb down the pipes," he thought nervously to himself.

But as he tried to clamber down, he was startled by Jordan, who, still hiding below, grabbed Steve's ankles.

"Got you!" he grinned.

Steve Strong put up a struggle, but by then the security guards had arrived and the place was surrounded. There was no escape for Steve now. Jordan and Steve descended the pipes and the stadium staff took Steve away. They took the medals back too. Steve wouldn't be getting any awards now, not even the silver. He'd been disqualified.

One of the officials led Jordan back to the main arena where a cheering crowd awaited him.

"We can now resume the award ceremony, thanks to our hero, the amazing Jumping Jordan," announced one of the officials. "Due to the disqualification of Steve Strong, Flexible Freddie will now receive the silver medal for second place."

Another of the officials exchanged Freddie's bronze medal for a dazzling silver one.

"This means that we have a new athlete in third place. Please give a huge round of applause for Sporty Sam!" the announcements continued.

Sporty Sam sprinted up to the podium and accepted his medal with great joy.

"And that just leaves us with the all-important glorious gold medal which I can now at last award to a most worthy winner. Please give a cheer for our champion, the amazing Jumping Jordan!"

The crowd exploded. They cheered, they roared, they waved their banners in the air. The applause echoed around the stadium. It was the greatest celebration the National Junior Athletics Championships had ever seen, and of course, the greatest moment of Jordan's life.

Tsunami Terror

By Vijai Lakshmanan

"Yay!" rejoiced Charlie. "I'm going to Gramma's."

Charlie keenly knocked on the door.

"Oh hello Charlie. I have your swimming kit. Your mum said it's your swimming day today," explained Gramma.

"Why? I don't want to go," protested Charlie.

"Charlie, it's very important to know how to swim, especially here in Hawaii where there are tsunamis almost every year."

Charlie sat on the stairs and folded his arms.

Gramma sat by his side and put her arm across his shoulders. "I want to tell you a story from when I was your age…"

Charlie listened.

"It had been an ordinary school day and I was walking home as usual, when suddenly, the weather

turned. The sky went dark and the wind began to blow furiously. Then it seemed as though a greyish-blue wall of water was moving towards me from the sea. It was a TSUNAMI!!!

"And this was no ordinary tsunami, it was a *mega* tsunami. The sky blushed with fear. It turned red as though it was going to explode. I ran for my life, whilst buildings crashed down as if in a war-zone. People were fleeing all over the place and crying out helplessly.

"It wasn't long before I was engulfed by an extremely long wave. Thankfully, I knew how to swim and, using all my strength, I escaped from the huge natural disaster." Gramma breathed deeply as she ended her story.

"That's astonishing, Gramma. How were you brave enough to swim in a tsunami? You could have drowned! Was the wave really that big?" Charlie was loaded with questions.

Gramma just smiled.

Now Charlie knew the significance of knowing how to swim. He jumped up from the stairs, grabbed his swimming kit and said,

"Ok, Gramma, let's go!"

Rescued

By Ahmed Pasha

As an explorer, it has always been in my blood to conquer new domains, and the volcano was next on my list. I insisted on going alone in spite of my colleagues' countless warnings that the volcano could erupt at any time. But I was feeling determined and possibly a little stubborn. So I closed my ears and walked away. I was going to board that helicopter and nothing was going to stop me.

Hovering above the majestic mountain, I slid off the helicopter and lowered myself down into the depths of the volcano. As soon as I touched down, I began searching for unusual specimens. Once I had gathered an impressive sample of rocks, I began my ascent.

As I climbed, some rocks crumbled, including the one my rope was tied to, and I fell. I yelled with anger and frustration because that was when I realised I was trapped and also hurt. I tried to radio for help but I couldn't get a signal on my tracker. At that point I began to worry. I was afraid I might die. And because there was no water, I drank my sweat; there was plenty of that, unpleasant though it was.

After several days, the volcano began to steam. If I had been an illustration in a comic, I would probably have appeared pale, with hair standing on end and my mouth wide open. There would also be a sign above me saying 'HORROR!' But at that exact second, the steam bloated my parachute and I flew!

I landed by some bushes which fortunately bore ripe berries and I ravenously devoured the fruit. Then, I heard a beep. Were my ears deceiving me? The beep came again. It was my tracker. It had connected. A signal. I was saved!

The rescue party found me during the early hours of the next morning and I felt the relief rush over me like a wave.

From then on, I knew I would be cautious and prepared, because from then on, I was more respectful of nature and less self-assured of my human powers over it.

The Fantastic Voyage

By Anisha Sirajudeen

It all began quite unexpectedly. Who would
have thought, me, a thin, fragile girl with no
extraordinary talent, could lead a voyage that would
be remembered for centuries?

It was on my thirteenth (unlucky for some)
birthday. My father, a caring man, had fallen
ill. He was a merchant and made his money
exporting valuable artefacts to other countries
or trading with collectors. However, his ships
couldn't travel without him and, without
father's income to pay the bills, we risked losing
our family home.

On the night of my birthday, my father
summoned me to his room to tell me something
important. He heaved himself up on the pillows of
his sickbed and spoke in a serious tone.

"Annie darling, I need you to do something

important for me. You might be alarmed. Are you ready?"

I nodded eagerly.

"You must lead the ships. It's the only way we can keep a roof over our heads..." he started to cough again.

"But what about mother?" I interrupted.

"I have checked with your mother and she's in agreement," Father replied.

I was gob-smacked. Never had I been given such a task. Would I succeed, or would I wreck everything? – including the ship! I knew it would be the question on everyone's lips.

During the days leading up to the voyage, my mother never left my side. Also, more frequently than ever before, I talked to my father. The voyage loomed nearer. I had never felt more nervous. But I had to do it, for my father, for my family, for the house and for our dignity.

I was taught, by a local sailor in Southampton, how to use the sextant and read the charts. His name was Alan. I had to say, "Ahoy Alan!" every time I saw him. However, I made up a name that would suit him better, 'Annoying Alan'. He was a hard task master.

I worked relentlessly but I always felt as if I was failing because he never gave me any words of encouragement. He just repeatedly barked orders and said, "Could be better, Missy." That annoyed me. Alan worked me harder and harder until I wondered if I'd have the strength to carry on.

There was a practice sail to the Isle of Wight to test my leadership skills and my ability to chart and stay on course. My mind and body were exhausted to the point where I stopped eating and couldn't sleep. At last, Alan gave me my license which meant he'd also given me his approval.

My mother packed me a chest full of clothes and all the food she could spare. Hugging me tightly, and holding back her tears, she whispered, "I wish I could come with you. But of course there's your father to take care of."

"I understand, Mother. This is something I must do alone. I will look on this as an opportunity," I replied.

The next morning, I felt proud as I left the house; I was about to do something no thirteen-year-old had done before. The inside of my stomach flipped when I saw the ship before me. A whole new adventure lay ahead – it was everything I'd trained for. It all seemed too much. But I remembered that this was my chance to prove myself, to me and the rest of the world. A chance to show that I was good for something. I could do it.

"For Father," I said, and I boarded the floating vessel. As we set sail I could hear my mother shouting, "Good luck Annie!" in the distance.

For five long days and nights we sailed until we reached the coast of Morocco, the island of my first trading station. The traders did not easily agree to my prices, but eventually I was able to bargain with them. I felt that I had more confidence than I'd started with, I did what I came to do and didn't fail. I never brought myself to thinking I would not complete the task successfully. It gave me a new lease of life. A better view of the true world outside. A fresh chapter.

As we travelled back, I was sitting in my cabin and charting our course, when I realised we were heading into a storm. Just as I made the discovery, the ship jerked sideways sharply. I ran up onto the deck to find that the men were all working hard to keep the ship afloat. I shouted commands which they understood.

I was unsure of what might happen, never before had I been caught in a storm. The ship buckled and swayed, pressured by the waves. The oars drove through the water. The hour was tense and frightening, never before had I faced such danger. But we got through it safely. I could see home in the distance. Home! Though it would still be a long night before we reached the harbour at Southampton.

As I climbed down from the ship, I felt I wasn't the same girl I started out as. I felt as if I had grown out of my own shadow. I left as a thirteen year old girl on the edge of childhood and I returned a young woman. My opinion of the world had altered; it was only a daunting place if you didn't have the courage to conquer it.

I hadn't just emotionally changed, I looked different. My cheeks, once pale, now had more colour and my body was stronger. My mother did the honour of hugging me first. Father's smile, when I caught sight of him at his window, suggested he was strengthened by the news of my accomplishments.

I had finished my sailing voyage, but my voyage into adulthood had just begun.

Journey to the Mountain of Peace

By Pavan Yadlapati

Long ago, in a barren land, lived Adam and his fellow villagers. They had always wanted to move to the Mountain of Peace because, year by year, the climate grew hotter and the land became drier.

One day, the king thought it was getting too hot and arranged a meeting to discuss the problem.

"Some of our bravest people must make an expedition to the Mountain of Peace," said the king seriously. "After they have explored it, they must return and escort our people there."

All of the villagers had a big discussion about who should go on the journey. Lots of people volunteered, but only six could go on the treacherous quest.

Adam was chosen to be the leader of the team. He picked five others; one navigator, one builder, two hunters and one experienced explorer who had been on other expeditions before. Each of the men packed a compass, a sword (just in case they encountered any beasts), a tent and a few of their own personal belongings.

Adam and his fine team set off to discover the Mountain of Peace. When they were almost halfway, night began to fall, so they tried to find a cave. After they travelled a bit further, they discovered one on the mountainside. The cave was empty so they went in and built a fire.

However, that was a big mistake because unbeknown to them, a bull lived in the cave. And it was no ordinary bull, it had serpents coming out of its head. The bull was a cross between Medusa and the Minotaur.

Adam's team drew their swords and fought very hard, but it was no use. They ran out of the cave and called to the almighty Zeus.

"Please, help us, Lord Zeus. Spare us from the jaws of this venomous beast!" they cried.

Zeus heard their prayers and struck the side of the mountain with a great lightning bolt. A huge boulder rolled down the mountainside and sealed the entrance to the cave. The beast, which had been weakened by the swordsmen, had not quite made it out of the cave and so remained trapped behind the boulder.

Adam and his fellow explorers heaved a huge sigh of relief and threw their arms up to the heavens to thank Zeus.

Exhausted by the battle, Adam and his men set up camp with the tents they had packed.

"We'd best use these for shelter from now on," suggested Adam. "Let's not risk any more caves."

"And let's hope the Mountain of Peace lives up to its name, when we finally discover it, and has no beasts such as the one we have just encountered," shivered one of the navigators. The men nodded in agreement.

The hunters went off in search of supper and soon returned with a catch of wild hare, which they roasted over a fire. As they ate, they reflected on the fight with the beast and told stories of their other adventures. After that, they settled down for a much needed good night's sleep.

The following morning, Adam and his men were ready. They set off to continue their expedition to the Mountain of Peace. When they were almost at the top, even though the men were weak and tired from their demanding journey, they were renewed with energy, knowing that they had almost reached their goal.

"Come on team! We're almost there!" cried Adam.

The travellers clambered to the top where they were met with the most wonderful sight. Such a beautiful spot with a stream running through it. Masses of vibrant flowers grew on the banks; there were daisies, buttercups and bluebells, to name but a few. Birds chattered and sang in the trees. A rainbow arched over the mountain as if to greet them.

That night, the hummingbirds filled the air with a peaceful melody, whilst a thousand stars glinted overhead. Adam rested in his tent, tired, yet proud to have discovered a new home for his villagers; he couldn't wait to share this discovery with them.

Danger at the Volcano

By Balraj Singh

Once there was a friendly, black dog called Ben. He lived in a village at the top of a mountain. He heard that the next mountain along was a volcano and he wanted to see it, so he set off on a journey.

Soon he found himself in a jungle. There he met a cheerful tiger.

"Where are you going?" enquired the tiger.

"I'm going to explore the volcano," explained Ben.

"Can I come?" asked the tiger.

"Yes you can," said Ben.

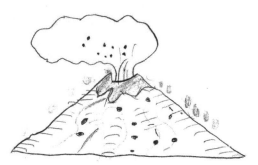

They journeyed together until they reached the foot of the volcano. Eager to explore, the tiger ran to the top.

"Be careful not to fall in!" warned Ben.

But the volcano was busy bubbling and burping so the tiger didn't hear him. Just as Ben had feared, the tiger toppled over the edge and fell inside.

The tiger dug his claws into the wall of the volcano and clung onto the rock. The hot fiery lava blazed below him.

"Help! Help!" cried the tiger.

Ben was frantic. He barked and barked and barked in the hope that he might attract some attention.

Something from somewhere deep down inside the volcano heard the tiger's cries and Ben's yelps. A golden fiery bird rose from the lava. It was a phoenix. The tiger was speechless. His mouth was wide open and his eyes almost bulged out of his head.

The phoenix flew up towards the tiger, gripped

his shoulders with his talons and lifted him into the air. They shot out of the top of the volcano like a rocket and landed in a nearby lake, which was a relief for the tiger as it cooled him down.

Ben came running down the side of the mountain. He swam across the lake and helped fish the tiger out. The phoenix swooped away towards the direction of the volcano.

"Oh, I wish it didn't have to fly off so soon, I never got a chance to say thank you," sighed the tiger.

"Oh well, at least we're safe," said Ben. "And I don't think we should go so close to the top of any volcanos ever again," he added.

"You can be sure of that!" wheezed the tiger.

How the Elephant got his Trunk

Retold by Adam Hakiem

Long ago, elephants didn't have trunks. Instead, they had a flabby bit of skin.

Once upon a time, in the Savannah of South Africa, Jack the elephant was playing foot-mango with his mates. Foot-mango is like football, but with a mango. As he was the top player, Jack kicked the mango fiercely. It landed in the swamp.

"Thanks a lot," groaned Jack's mates. Everyone knew that what went into the swamp was lost

FOREVER. This was because a terrible croc lived there and he loved all young flesh, including Jack's. So the elephants went to get another mango from the jungle.

However, when they got there, they found no mangoes. Instead there was only a dried up mango tree rotting away in the dead jungle.

"Oh no! We must warn the others," cried Jack. When they returned, the Savannah was also dry. The lush shrubs, the stream and the trees, apart from their gnarled stubs, were all gone. It was doom-like. The only water left, was in Croc's swamp.

Jack and his friends were terrified. How were they meant to collect water for the tree without getting snapped by Croc? They huddled up and put their ginormous brains together.

"I've got it!" the wisest of the elephants exclaimed. "We'll hide in a bush, and then Jack, you'll creep out, check if the coast is clear and take a drink from the swamp while Croc isn't looking."

"How am I meant to know when he's not looking?" said Jack.

"Just drink quickly," advised the wisest.

They waited till dusk, when the mist hung low. Then Jack crept out of the bush and looked around cautiously. He dipped his flabby snout silently into the swamp and began to drink.

Jack hadn't realised that Croc was actually

lurking in the reeds, stalking his target. Croc snapped at Jack and bit his flab.

"Aaaaaaarrrrrrgggggghhhh!" Jack yelled.

This brought all his friends running from the bush. The flabby skin began to stretch as Croc pulled at it with his chompers. The wisest of the elephants grabbed Jack's tail and pulled. The others formed a line, held on to each other, and they too pulled and pulled with all their might. Croc let go and they all fell backwards onto the ground.

When they got up they were amazed. They had all pulled so hard, that Jack's flab had become astonishingly long. All the elephants loved it, so one by one they got Croc to stretch their flab as well. In all the excitement, Jack trumpeted the most joyous sound from his newly stretched hooter. And so, they named it TRUNK!

Ant's Adventure

By Anban Senthil Prabu

Where am I? What is this place? Am I all alone? As Ant ventured through the green wilderness, his mind overflowed with questions.

Ant was a young, shy insect who preferred to be with his family rather than where he'd ended up. He had fallen from the flower that was his home and was now lost. With all the towering grass that surrounded him, it seemed to Ant as if he was in a jungle. He was in fact simply in an ordinary country park, but as he was so tiny, he was completely overwhelmed.

Ant wandered hopelessly through the endless green, everywhere he turned he found himself stumbling over lumps of earth. He walked up the sloping blades of grass, only to be flung back again.

After a few hours, which to Ant seemed like years, he came across an enormous oak tree, so tall it disappeared into the clouds. Dazed by this extreme sight, Ant stared at the tree for ages without blinking. He had to shake his head vigorously to bring himself back to his senses.

Ant, after thinking for some time, decided to climb the tree. Maybe he could get a bird's eye view of the area from up there, rather than stumbling through nothing but grass. Ant struggled up through the bark, the rough ridges and bumps made it quite a challenge. He almost lost his grip several times, though he was determined to keep going.

As night fell, Ant began to feel drowsy. He could hardly keep his head up, and almost nodded off completely several times. Ant realised he needed to rest and decided to drag himself to the nearest branch and settle down for the night. He found a comfortable resting place on a leaf.

Ant had been snoozing for about an hour or so, when a ferocious, raging storm broke out. Unfortunately for Ant, who was in the middle of a never-ending dream, he was swept away by the wind on his green leaf. Caught up in the swishing, swirling, tumbling, turning storm, Ant spiralled downwards. Remarkably, Ant was so worn out, he somehow managed to sleep through the whole thing. It was a miracle he didn't fall off the leaf.

When Ant awoke to find that he wasn't on the branch but stuck on a lake, his weariness was replaced with worry. Panting heavily, Ant frantically looked around for a way out of the mess he'd found himself in.

He was startled by a sudden quack.

A curious duck swam over to the leaf. "Oh, an ant! What a surprise. What brings you to this pond, of all places?" she enquired.

"I'm lost!" whimpered Ant softly.

The duck was concerned for the little ant. In a motherly voice she said, "Well then, we need to get you home. How about climbing on my back?"

Ant wiped away a tear, looked up and nodded. The duck happily lowered her feathery wings and allowed Ant to climb on her back. Ant, after making himself all cosy in her feathers, told the duck of his home – a towering plant with a giant head, almost like a sunflower, though with blue petals.

The duck lifted her vast wings and soared into the sky. Once they were up in the air, Ant spotted out of the corner of his eye, a beautiful tall plant with blue petals.

"Home!" cried Ant.

The duck turned and saw it too. She dived down at a mind-blowing speed and made a swift landing. Ant jumped off.

Ant's entire colony came out to see what the commotion was about and there he was... Ant! Everyone ran towards him and hugged him as if he was a long lost relative, which in fact, he was.

Ant, after all the hugs and kisses, cleared his throat and explained everything. When he had finished, he looked up at the duck and proclaimed, "This is my great loyal friend. If it wasn't for her, I wouldn't be here. I insist she stays for dinner."

All the other ants happily agreed, although they secretly wondered what on earth they might feed her. The duck looked down at Ant with a gentle smile, knowing they would be best friends forever.

Foxilla

By Lily Beglin

One sunny day, a baby fox was born and she was named Foxilla. But she wasn't an ordinary fox. She had a magical power which meant she could turn invisible. I'm going to tell you about the day when she found out about it. So are you comfy? Good, then let's get started.

One day, when Foxilla was living her nice ordinary life (well an ordinary life for a fox, that is), a mean, tall hunter came along. He wanted to catch a fox for his wife. She loved wearing the fur around her shoulders. First, he had to find the fox's lair.

Sitting in her foxhole deep in the heart of the woods, Foxilla sensed danger as the hunter's footsteps approached. Foxilla was scared and didn't know what to do. However, she tried to stay calm because if she panicked the hunter would hear her and hunt her down. So what she did was, she tried to be strong and think positive thoughts. She thought about her family, she imagined herself to be the bravest fox in the land and she believed in her heart that she would survive. As she did so, she felt a strange tingling sensation running through her spine and all the way to the tip of her tail.

Still, the hunter approached her den. He was so close Foxilla could smell his rotten boots. He peered into her hideout. Now they were face to face. She was definitely for it. Foxilla shivered with terror.

But the hunter just sniffed a little, scratched his chin and frowned. After a few moments, to Foxilla's surprise, the hunter stepped away in confusion. How had he not noticed her? Why hadn't he taken a shot?

Foxilla looked down at her paws to find that she couldn't see them! It was then that she realised she was invisible! It was a miracle!

She crept quietly past the mean, tall hunter and walked away from her home, sad in the thought that she would never be able to return, as the hunter would surely be back. She travelled so far that when she eventually stopped, she realised she was in a completely different environment. No longer a wood, but a village. She looked around and noticed a sign that told her she was in a place called County Land.

It was very quiet there. Foxilla approached a charming little cottage. It had a red roof with white polka-dots, rather like a toadstool. Foxilla knocked on the door and a little, cute fox answered.

"Is your mother home?" asked Foxilla.

The little, cute fox replied, "Yes, would you like to speak to her?"

Foxilla replied, "Yes I would, if you don't mind."

So the little fox's mother arrived at the door. She and Foxilla had a chat. Foxilla explained how she was now homeless because of the mean, tall hunter. Foxilla then burst into tears.

Mother Fox rested a gentle paw on Foxilla's shoulder and said reassuringly, "It's alright dearie, you can live with us."

Foxilla trotted happily into the house and immediately felt

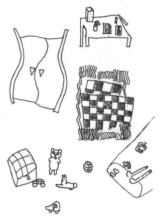

at home. When Mother Fox gave her some dinner, Foxilla realised just how hungry she was. She ate quite quickly, but at the same time, remembered to be polite.

Day turned into evening and Foxilla felt exhausted after all the drama, as well as from all the walking. So Mother Fox showed Foxilla to her new bed, where she curled up contentedly with the little, cute fox, knowing that at last she was safe.

Captured!

By Neelay Kawol

Once upon a time, on a farm, there lived a horse and a dog who were both great friends.

One day, a man ran into the field. He did not look friendly at all. He had green and black hair and cuts and bruises all over his hands. He was a stranger and the dog knew he was up to no good.

"Woof!" the dog barked at him.

The man had a box with a picture of a dog on it and before the dog knew it, the man had given him something that made him feel sleepy. He caught the dog and trapped him inside the box.

Later the dog woke up and found that he was in a cage with people staring at him.

"Woof!" cried the dog anxiously. He looked around to find that the horse was beside him in another cage. The strange man must have captured him too. The horse stomped his feet angrily and scratched the ground roughly. More and more faces peered at them through the cages. Everyone was interested in the horse more than the dog because of the fuss it was making. The strange man returned and gave the horse something to make it feel sleepy again, and so he calmed down.

At night time, when all the people had gone, someone whispered to the horse and the dog from the next cage along. It was a lion. The lion said to the dog and the horse, "I've had enough. I've been here for a whole year."

"You've got big strong teeth," said the horse. "Why don't you try cutting the bars?"

The lion tried with all its might and after a great effort, he broke through his cage.

"That was awesome," whispered the dog. "Now do ours too."

The lion ripped through the dog's cage, then the horse's as well.

They ran through the city for hours. They got so hungry that they ate food from the dustbins.

"Where are we?" said the dog. "How are we ever going to find home?"

The dog, the horse and the lion climbed up a giant hill so they could get a good view of the area. Beyond them stretched several fields.

"That looks like our farm!" exclaimed the dog.

"Yes, I can see the big barn and the windmill," cried the horse.

The three animals raced across the land in the direction of the farm. When they arrived, everything was as it had always been. All their friends welcomed them back. There were five ducks, two cows and eleven sheep.

"Who's your new friend?" asked one of the ducks.

"This is the lion we met on our adventure," said the dog. "He helped us to escape."

"But why does he look sad?" asked a sheep.

"I am all alone and have no home anymore," sighed the lion.

"Don't be silly," said the horse. "We are your friends now and you can live in the barn."

"As long as you promise not to eat us!" said the ducks.

"I would never dream of eating my new friends," said the lion.

Everybody laughed and they lived a jolly life on the farm for the rest of their days.

Journey to Namibia

By Rehaan Gupta Chaudhary

One sunny day in Algeria, in Africa, there lived a giraffe called Jim. His habitat was a desert which was getting hotter every year, the water was drying up and the trees were dying. Poor Jim was always hungry and thirsty. He knew he had to find a better place to live.

He decided to travel to Namibia because he had heard of an amazing place for animals there called the Etosha National Park. So he set off on his long journey.

Along the way, he stopped at Kenya to drink some water and feed on some leaves. He decided to have a rest under a nearby tree. When he woke up, he was ready to continue on his way.

After several days of travelling, Jim sensed something unusual happening; the sky went a blackish purple, the wind blew eerily through the trees and the earth began to tremor. Stones rattled and scattered along the ground. Suddenly, there was an almighty bang and a tremendous crack. To Jim's horror, he realised it was an earthquake.

The ground split in two, swallowing everything in its path – stones, small creatures and even trees! Jim was terrified and he raced, almost as fast as a cheetah, to a mountain and began to climb it.

When he looked around, he became worried because he realised he was lost; the earthquake had destroyed the only path he knew.

"Hello, do you need any help?"

"Who said that?" wondered Jim, who had thought he was alone.

A zebra stepped out of the trees and went over to talk to him.

"You look lost. Where are you trying to get to?"

"I need to get to Namibia," replied Jim.

"Follow me. I know the way," offered the zebra.

They journeyed over the mountains, across Tanzania, through Zambia and past Botswana, until they finally reached Namibia.

"Wow! It's beautiful," marvelled Jim.

They had arrived at the Etosha National Park. There were lots of animals roaming free, such as zebras, elephants and all sorts of birds, including ostriches. Many of them lived by the salt pan. Even though Namibia was partly desert, the Etosha National Park was full of vegetation.

Jim spotted other giraffes grazing at the Mapani trees and trotted over to join them.

"Who are you?" asked one of the giraffes.

"My name is Jim. I have come from Algeria to seek a better home," he explained.

"You are most welcome here," said the other giraffe.

Jim beckoned his zebra companion over and introduced him to his new friends.

As he munched contentedly on the leaves of the Mapani trees, Jim knew he had at last found the home he had been looking for.

The Foolish Forester

By Sacha Doherty

Down in the deep, dark forest, a woodsman, who had never acted in kindness, was up to his usual selfish deeds. He was about to cut down yet another set of trees so he could sell the timber for a pile of money.

He didn't care for the orangutans who made the forest their habitat. As he hacked away at their home, he just smiled. When he had finished his work, he looked back over his shoulder, chuckled, turned again and went on his way.

The distressed orangutans huddled together to keep warm, but the babies couldn't stop shivering because they were so small and they cried all through the night.

In the nearby village, lived a boy called Miko. He was a bold boy. He wasn't exactly rude, but the other villagers often commented on his lively behaviour.

One day, he was strolling through the forest when he spotted the homeless orangutans huddling together in the barren wasteland that the forester had left behind. They were looking rather sorry for themselves. Miko felt worried because he had never seen these creatures looking this way. They were usually hanging from the trees, playing and swinging joyfully. But now, there were no were trees, just the remains of the foolish forester's devastation.

As Miko approached them to take a closer look, the youngest orangutan ambled towards him. Even though the orangutan was tired, he gave Miko a cheeky grin. Miko liked him instantly because he reminded him of himself.

As Miko was getting to know the orangutans, he heard the sound of a truck. It was the woodsman returning. The orangutans started pointing at the truck and shrieking.

"What is it, my furry friends?" asked Miko.

He watched as the woodsman climbed out of his truck and collected up more of the timber from the forest floor.

Most of the orangutans fled, but the youngest, whom Miko liked the best, stayed.

"Ah, I see now. Is this the foolish forester who tore down your home?"

The young orangutan nodded wildly and continued pointing at the truck.

Miko was furious. He pulled out a piece of paper and a pencil from his pocket. He looked more closely at the truck and made a note of the number plate. He wouldn't approach the forester directly, he would give the information to the community leader instead.

When the woodsman eventually drove away, the rest of the orangutans returned. They all hugged Miko with relief.

"I must leave you now," explained Miko, "but I promise to report the foolish forester to the authorities and see that he doesn't get away with this."

There was a big meeting going on in the main village that evening, because the community were choosing a new leader. Miko turned up just as he was being elected. He put his hand up to get the leader's attention.

"Yes, boy. What can I do for you?" asked the leader.

Miko bravely stepped up to the front. He put his hand in his pocket and pulled out the piece of paper with the foolish forester's number plate details.

"What's this?" frowned the leader.

"I need to report a serious crime," said Miko boldly. "There's a vile man who comes to our beautiful forest and chops down the trees to sell. He is destroying nature and the homes of a family of orangutans. All for money!"

Everyone in the room gasped.

"Have you any evidence?" questioned the leader.

"Yes," said Miko, unfolding the piece of paper and showing it to the leader. "This is the forester's details. All you have to do is trace this number. I got it from his truck."

"Well done. Leave this with me, we'll deal with it right away."

After the meeting, the leader worked with the authorities to track down the woodsman. They found him sitting outside his hut at the edge of the forest counting his money. Beside him was the truck and it was loaded with tree trunks ready to be carted off to the merchants.

"Caught you red handed!" proclaimed the leader.

"Alright, I know it was wrong, but I was only doing it to make a living," confessed the foolish forester.

Two officers, hand-cuffed him. He wriggled uncomfortably, but accepted that he must face the consequences.

He was sent to court and made to pay a fine. The judge also said that the foolish forester must return to the woods to reflect on the damage he had caused.

The woodsman did as he was told and when he arrived, he found the family of orangutans cowering under one of the few trees that was left. All around them were dead tree stumps and dried leaves. The forester felt truly ashamed of himself and sorry for what he had done.

Using the last of the wood that was still on his truck, he quickly set to work and built a wonderful enclosure for the Orangutans. At first they were suspicious of the forester, but eventually they understood he was trying to make amends. When their new habitat was finished, and they saw just how homely it was, they all rushed in and rejoiced. The cheeky one leapt and bounced all around, squealing and chattering with delight.

Miko strode up to see what the forester had done. He stood there admiring his handiwork. It was clear now that he was no longer a foolish forester, but a fantastic forester.

Ben's Quest for the Magic Key

By Ariana Khan

One day, a dog called Roe was playing catch in a field with his friend Ben, who was a horse. Roe passed the ball to Ben but he missed it and the ball went over the fence. Ben went to get it but his head got stuck in the fence because the gap was too small.

Roe went to help Ben out of the fence. He tugged and tugged at his mane but he would not budge. Then a mysterious voice came out of nowhere.

"This is the voice of the magic fence. Now you are stuck, you are in my powers."

Roe and Ben could not believe their ears.

"Why would you want to do that?" asked Roe.

The fence replied, "It's not much fun being stuck in the ground all day. I need something to keep me amused."

"But that's not fair," said Roe. "Ben can't stay here forever. How will he eat or sleep?"

"Well, there *is* something you can do," said the fence.

"What is it?" asked Ben. "We'll do anything."

"You need a magic key to break the spell," explained the fence.

"Do you know where the key is?" asked Ben.

"Yes. It's embedded in a block of wood that's kept in a secret room," said the mysterious voice.

"But where *is* this secret room?" asked Ben whose neck was beginning to ache.

"In the middle of the forest," replied the fence.

"I'll go right now," said Roe.

"Don't be too long" said Ben.

"I'll do my best," said Roe, and off he went.

As Roe entered the forest he came across a bird who was cheeping in distress because one of her babies had fallen down from her nest. She was a woodpecker and she was very worried about her baby. Roe gently scooped up the tiny bird in his paws and put it back where it belonged.

"Thank you. If I can ever help you in return just whistle," said the woodpecker.

"I will," said Roe. "Goodbye for now." He waved farewell to the woodpecker and continued on his way.

Eventually Roe came across a small grey castle in the middle of the forest. He pushed open a creaky wooden door and made his way through several dusty corridors in search of the secret room where the block of wood with the magic key in it was.

Just as he was about to enter the correct room, he heard a voice cry, "Stop!"

Roe turned to find a giant cat wearing a golden crown standing behind him.

"Ah, I bet I know who's sent you," winked the cat. "It's that old spirit of the fence up to his tricks again, isn't it?"

"How do you know about that?" asked Roe.

"We're a team, that's what we are."

"But why would you want to play such horrid tricks?" frowned Roe. "My poor friend is trapped back there in that fence and his neck must be really hurting by now."

"Well, I'm stuck here in this dusty old castle all the time, so I need something to keep me amused."

"If you say so," said Roe. "But it's still not fair and I really must have the magic key now."

"Be my guest," grinned the cat, showing Roe into the secret room.

Roe realised why the cat was laughing, when he saw where the key was. It was jammed so deep in the block of wood, he had no chance of getting the key out.

"Ha ha, your friend is trapped forever!" cackled the cat.

But then Roe had an idea. "That's what *you* think," he said.

Roe stood on his hind legs and whistled and whistled and whistled.

The cat didn't know what to think. It seemed Roe had gone crazy. Just then, the woodpecker who Roe had helped earlier, whooshed through the window and got  to work immediately on the block of wood. She pecked away at the bark so quickly that Roe and the cat could hardly see her amidst the blurry, whirly rush of activity. Soon there was nothing left of the woodblock, except for a pile of sawdust, on top of which lay the magic key.

Roe picked up the key, laughed at the very fed up looking cat, thanked the woodpecker and rushed out of the castle. He ran through the forest and back to the field where his friend, Ben the horse, was still stuck in the fence.

"Thank goodness you're back," cried Ben. "Have you got the key?"

"I most certainly have," smiled Roe.

The voice of the enchanted fence gasped, "I don't believe it!"

Roe fitted the magic key into a knot in the wood and the fence clattered to the ground in pieces.

"Phew, thank goodness for that," said Ben, stretching his sore neck from side to side. "However did you manage to get hold of the key?" he asked.

"It's a long story," said Roe. "I'll tell you later. But in the meantime, let's keep away from any crooked fences, hey?"

And the two friends trotted off to another field where they could play more safely.

The Rabbit and the Magic Portal

By Alishbah Atif

There was once a rabbit with the fluffiest grey fur anyone had ever seen.

One bright sunny day, the rabbit was thinking about going to the meadow to play in the grass and hop about amongst the hills.

"Please can you let me go to the meadow? Pretty please," she asked her mummy politely.

"NO I CAN'T LET YOU"! yelled her mummy.

The fluffy rabbit shivered and shook. She was so upset that some

of her fluffy fur fell off. She ran into her fluffy bedroom, buried her head in her fluffy pillow and cried.

After a while, she lay back on her fluffy bed and looked out through the window. She could see the flowery meadow. She was so desperate to go there. She turned to face the wall. The wall began to shimmer and a magic mysterious door appeared. She touched the door and her hand went through it. She stepped forwards and found herself going completely through the door.

She was outside! But she was not in the meadow as expected, she was in the middle of a forest.

She turned back to return to the safety of her house but it was no longer there.

Just ahead of her stood a tall tree, and in the trunk of the tree there was a door. It was bright yellow and had a honey pot painted on it. It looked jolly enough, so she went up and knocked on the door.

A friendly bee answered. She had a red bow on her head and a lovely big smile.

"You look as if you've been crying. What's the problem, rabbit?"

"My meadow it's... it's... it's not there!" the rabbit stammered and sniffled.

"That's because you've come through the magic portal. That shimmering door was no ordinary door. It leads to new lands and adventures," the bee explained.

The rabbit was speechless. She liked the idea of an adventure, but she also hoped she would be able to get back home. Her mummy might have shouted at her earlier, but she still loved her and was beginning to miss her. She didn't like the look of the dark forest. She preferred the meadow.

"Try not to feel anxious," said the bee. "I tell you what, why don't I make us some tea with toast and honey, and then I can show you the way back to the magic portal?"

The bee led the rabbit inside and gave her some tissues, then they sat down to the tea and toast.

After that, the rabbit was feeling much better. "Thank you, that was delicious, but I really would like to be getting back to my mummy now," she said.

The rabbit leapt off the sofa and peeked outside. In the distance, through the woods and the trees, the scene began to shimmer again.

"There you go. Can you see that clearing over there?" said the bee. "If you go through the shimmering trees, it will lead you back home."

"Thank you very much," said the rabbit, and she scampered off towards the magic portal.

The rabbit stepped through the shimmery clearing and found herself back in her fluffy bedroom. There was a knock at the door. It was her mummy.

"I'm sorry I shouted at you earlier. It's just that I was so busy and tired and I had a headache. But it's ok now. Let's have a nice hug and then we can go together to the meadow."

The rabbit felt glad that everything was alright and, after a comforting hug, they hopped off together and had a lovely afternoon in the beautiful grassy meadow.

Flossie Learns her Lesson

By Deeqa Mohamed

There was once a pony called Flossie. She had a glossy peach-coloured coat with a dappled neck, and a mane that flowed like angel's hair, just like her mother's. However, unlike her mother, she was also really naughty and cheeky.

"Come to our beautiful garden, it has wonderful flowers blooming in it today," said her mother.

"No! I will not come. It is ugly, not beautiful," Flossie said. She was just being silly. It wasn't really an ugly garden at all.

"You are such a rude little pony!" scolded Flossie's mother.

"I don't care!" said Flossie and she ran off into the forest.

The forest floor was thick with twigs and Flossie found it very difficult to run. Whilst she was dragging her hooves through the rough ground,

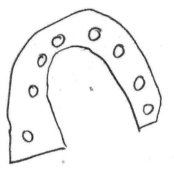

one of them got caught in her horseshoe and her shoe came off.

"Ouch!" cried Flossie. It really hurt not having a shoe.

She limped all the way back to find her mum in the garden. It was a long, slow, painful journey for Flossie. Along the way she had time to think.

When she found her mother she went up to her to apologise. "I'm really sorry about running off. I know now that I need you."

Her mother was kind and easily forgave Flossie. "Let's get you to the blacksmith's and fix that shoe of yours."

"Thank you Mother. From now on I will always listen to you and never be cheeky or naughty again," said Flossie.

"We'll see about that," chuckled her mother.

And the two ponies happily trotted off together.

The Rabbit, the Horse, the Woods and the Castle

By Raja Khalid

There was once a rabbit and a horse who lived in a wood. However, the wood was too dangerous for them because their home risked being damaged by storms.

So they left to go to the castle to meet the Queen to see if she could offer them a safer place to stay. To their delight, she allowed them to stay in the castle grounds, as long as they worked for her.

One day, the Queen told them to get wood for the fire, so they had to go back to the forest. Suddenly a great storm broke out. Thunder roared through the skies and lightning struck the trees, causing the branches to catch fire.

From her tower, the Queen noticed the flames in the distance and realised that the rabbit and the horse could be in danger.

"Heeeeeeeelllllpppp!!!!!" cried the rabbit and the horse.

Their cries were carried by the wind in the direction of the castle. Now the Queen knew for sure that they were in trouble, so she sent all of her knights, except the weak ones, to help. They galloped into the woods, rescued the rabbit and the horse and brought them safely back to the castle.

However, the rabbit and the horse still hadn't got any wood for the fire.

"Where IS the wood!" shouted the Queen. She was so cross she threatened to throw them out of the castle.

"Sorry, we dropped all the firewood in the storm," apologised the rabbit.

"Please give us one more chance, please," begged the horse.

"Ok, only if you stop snivelling and promise to do better next time," ordered the Queen.

"Of course," agreed the rabbit and the horse.

"That fireplace is not going to work itself is it?" continued the Queen.

So, the next time the rabbit and the horse went to gather wood, they made sure to look at the sky first to check that there were no clouds or lightning bolts to be seen.

Over time, they got much better at gathering wood for the castle and so were able to stay there comfortably and happily forever more.

The Leaping Lion

By Camron Dhillon

Once upon a time there lived a leaping lion named Ben. He had a fiery, red mane and beautiful, sunset-coloured fur.

Ben's job was to help other animals to travel if they wanted to go on holiday. He was proud of his job, but he wanted a holiday of his own too. So he saved up until he had enough money.

When he managed to pay for his trip, he was extremely happy. "YIPPEE!" he cried, and he packed his bags and headed off for the airport.

When he was on the aeroplane he had to wait and wait. "This is boring," he muttered. Finally the plane took off and Ben was very excited by the view from the window because he could see the sea. But when the plane was landing it messed up Ben's ears, so he chewed on a piece of gum.

Once the plane had arrived, Ben leapt off and

looked around. "Wow!" There was a beautiful sandy beach with the brightest blue sea beyond it.

Ben had a 'To Do' list. The first thing he had to do was to find a hotel to stay in. He strolled up to the best hotel on the beach.

"Hello, I would like the finest room that you have in this hotel," he asked the man at the desk.

While Ben was wandering through the corridor to find his room, he came across a strange wolf with fur so silvery, it was almost transparent.

"Would you be able to tell me where Room 42 is please?" Ben asked the wolf.

"Carry on going straight, then turn left," replied the mysterious wolf.

"Thanks," said Ben. He did exactly as the wolf had instructed and found his room. He unpacked his animal suitcase, put on his swimming trunks and headed straight for the beach.

Ben climbed onto some rocks, eager to dive into the sea, but when he looked down, he saw a hungry shark waiting for him.

"Boy, you look good for supper," grinned the shark, flashing his huge, white teeth.

Ben smiled nervously and backed away.

"Phew that was a close one," shuddered Ben. "But I still have a big problem. How am I going to have a nice swim in the sea?"

At that moment, the mysterious silvery wolf came creeping softly across the sand. He stood on the highest rock that jutted out over the sea and howled a hypnotic song across the waves.

The sea began to swirl. The shark got caught up in the whirlpool and began to spin. He got so dizzy, he forgot all about feeling hungry, instead he felt extremely seasick. So he swam giddily away back to the depths of the ocean where he'd come from.

Ben leapt up to the rock where the silvery wolf stood and prepared to dive into the sea. Before he made his big splash, he turned to thank the wolf, but the wolf was no longer there.

"I wonder where he went?" thought Ben. "I was going to ask him if he wanted to join me. Ah well, here goes!"

Ben leapt off the rock, dove into the water and had the best swim ever!

Flour Shower

By Max Currie

After school, Rahama came round to Max's house to play. Whilst having had a brilliant time on the Xbox, they began to feel hungry, so they went into the kitchen where Max's mum was dancing around to the radio.

"Yo, Mum, can we have some pizza please?" asked Max.

"How about we make one together?" suggested Mum.

"Yay!" cheered Max.

"Yum!" exclaimed Rahama.

When they got the ingredients out of the cupboards and the fridge they realised they didn't have any pepperoni or sausage.

"We can just have cheese and tomato then," said Mum.

"NO!" complained Max. "You know how much I like my pepperoni and sausage."

"Ok," sighed Mum. "I'll just pop out to the shop. I won't be a jiffy. Make sure you don't open the door to anyone. And *be* good!"

Once Mum had left, Max and Rahama found themselves sitting around in the kitchen with nothing to do. They soon got bored.

"Why don't we make the dough?" Max suggested.

"Shouldn't we wait for your mum to get home?" worried Rahama.

But Max was already reaching for the bowl and flour. He tipped the flour in the bowl and it puffed back into his face. Rahama thought it was funny and burst into hysterics.

"Ha ha!" he cried.

Max got annoyed and blew a handful of flour back in Rahama's face.

A full flour fight then developed. Their hair looked as if they'd had a pillow fight and all the feathers had stuck to their heads and their faces were so white, they looked like mime artists. The kitchen itself was covered with flour. They both thought it was hilarious.

But when Mum returned home she wasn't so pleased. "What a dreadful mess you've made!" said Mum dropping her shopping bags. "Tidy it!"

As Max and Rahama apologetically scrubbed away, Mum realised they were trying their best, so she helped them. However, when they were finished, they were super tired and didn't feel like making pizza anymore. The boys were keen to get out of the kitchen and just wanted to lay down on the sofa and play Xbox.

"Why don't we order Papa John's instead?" Mum proposed.

"Yes! That's the best idea ever, how did we not think of that in the first place?" Max and Rahama chuckled.

Story of a Storyteller

By Siddarth Sridhar

Guess who I am. I am a book. Quite happy to be one actually. I think. I spend day and night, cosy and warm on my bookshelf, next to my neighbours who kindly share the space with me. However, I anxiously look down every day in hope of a new owner and sigh melancholically as the shop closes and I lie down for another night in my tight compartment.

Today I feel hopeful. This is the day. I'm itching my dusty pages with a dry splinter, when a broad figure with long, blonde hair strides briskly into the shop. The book I'm made of says that these beings are called 'women'.

I eagerly watch as she scrolls through the shelves. The woman does this until she's right in front of me. This is it! She reaches out her slim arm in my direction. But then she turns and grabs the book on my right. I shrink beneath my cover in despair. Another day on the bookshelf.

At night, when the store is closed, I think about the wretched day I've had. It should have been me. *I* should be the one travelling to new places. What's wrong with me? Why am I being neglected? Why does no one pick me? So many questions that will remain unanswered throughout the night.

I spring to attention at the click of a switch, the next morning. Time flies. Maybe I'd stayed up too late last night. My misery still remains and I don't dare look forwards. But the shrill pounding of footsteps tempts me. I can't restrain my sense of hope and I eagerly turn my head towards the entrance. No one? I look again. Nothing. This is utterly peculiar, as there should be at least one person browsing the stash of books. I'm sure I heard footsteps.

Frantically I look down to see that there *is* someone lurking around. It is a teenage boy. However, he isn't looking for books, he's staring at a miniscule gadget. People call it 'Smartphone'. I mean if you're coming to a bookstore where you can find wonderful books, like me for instance, why just sluggishly kick back on some stupid gadget?

I exhale deeply. My pages sink and I wonder what will happen to me in time. This is nothing like what my ancestors went through. They lived a full life. Back in the day, books were the only source of joy. Now there's technology. Maybe, in time we will be erased and... will be no more!

My mind is clouded with thoughts as I continue glaring at the boy surmounted by an interactive world, activated by a single tiny tap. Why must I be a book?

The boy is all I think about, whilst my shelf companions rest without torment. The thought, that I might be no more, stays in my mind and never leaves, worrying me constantly.

The next day, my enthusiasm perishes and I moan in desolation. The boy is not there today. Just a couple of people scanning the books. I don't even look up. I'm so miserable, I don't care. Suddenly, a wrinkled hand reaches out for me, and plucks me from my shelf. Can this really be? I pinch my cover to make sure. I wake abruptly. It is the middle of the night. It had indeed been too good to be true.

I listen to my neighbours chatting, intrigued by their conversation.

"Did you know that my friend got picked by someone earlier today?" one of them says.

"I feel so happy for him!" the other exclaims.

"It's getting harder these days for someone to come by your shelf and reach out their hand for you," his neighbour sighs.

"Indeed," the other mumbles.

Deep in thought, I silently contemplate our plight. What makes one book different from another?

The next morning, I gaze across the store. There's a boy skulking around. He looks familiar. I realise he's the boy who was in the other day. The one who kept on browsing on his gadget. But this time, he isn't carrying his phone. He's wandering in search of books!

I think for a second, whether he has been hit by a coconut or something, but then he takes out a damaged Smartphone from his pocket. So that's why!

All of a sudden, my cover begins to feel itchy. The itch grows until it becomes unbearable. I feel so scratchy I rip my cover from myself. I look so different without it. Could it be? This isn't my cover at all! I've been something else all along! The boy turns in my direction. He clambers up to the top shelf. He inspects me, his blue eyes all a shimmer.

"A book on gadgets!" he gasps.

Our faces meet. He reaches out and clutches me. I am filled with glee as he takes me away. I bid farewell to my old home as I watch it disappear in the distance.